Fred Rogers PRODUCTIONS

Donkey Hodie™

A P... Planet Purple

MW01097895

Adapted by May Nakamura
Based on the screenplay "Planet Purple Party"
written by Adam Rudman and David Rudman

Simon Spotlight

New York London Toronto Sydney New Delhi

SIMON SPOTLIGHT
An imprint of Simon & Schuster Children's Publishing Division
1230 Avenue of the Americas, New York, New York 10020
This Simon Spotlight paperback edition May 2022
© 2022 The Fred Rogers Company.
Donkey Hodie is produced by Fred Rogers Productions and Spiffy Pictures.
All rights reserved, including the right of reproduction in whole or in part in any form.
SIMON SPOTLIGHT and colophon are registered trademarks of Simon & Schuster, Inc.
For information about special discounts for bulk purchases, please contact Simon &
Schuster Special Sales at 1-866-506-1949 or business@simonandschuster.com.
Manufactured in the United States of America 0322 LAK
2 4 6 8 10 9 7 5 3 1
ISBN 978-1-6659-1342-3 (pbk)
ISBN 978-1-6659-1343-0 (ebook)

It was a special day in **Someplace Else**. Purple Panda was preparing for Mama Panda's birthday! Donkey Hodie was giving her a purple flower as a present.

"Hi, Purple Panda! I can't wait to go to your mama's birthday party!" Donkey Hodie said.

"Me too!" Purple Panda replied. "Get ready because we're going to fly my spaceship all the way to **Planet Purple** to bring the party to Mama! I have a birthday card for her and a cake and a lot of other things to bring. It's going to be a great party!"

Donkey and Panda climbed inside the spaceship.

"We can't be late to the party," Panda said. Then he looked at his "Start the Spaceship and Blast Off" list. The list always helped him remember how to prepare the spaceship for blastoff.

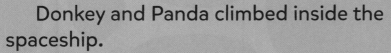

The first item on the "Start the Spaceship and the Blast Off" list was to buckle up. Panda and Donkey both buckled their seat belts.

The second item on the list was to push the big purple button and turn on the spaceship. Donkey and Panda pressed the button together.

The third and last item on the list was to count down. Donkey and Panda chanted together:

3...2...1...

BLAST OFF!

The spaceship soared toward Planet Purple.

"I can't wait to give Mama my special big birthday card," Panda said.

Donkey looked to her left. Then she looked to her right. "Hey . . . where is the birthday card?" she asked.

"Oh no!" Panda said. He had forgotten to bring the card with him!

"Let's turn this ship around!" Donkey declared. Panda landed the spaceship back on Someplace Else and hurriedly grabbed the big birthday card.

Donkey and Panda buckled up, pushed the big purple button, and counted down again.

3 . . . 2 . . . 1!

Soon the spaceship was blasting off into the sky again—this time, with the big birthday card also on board!

Finally, Panda felt sure that he had remembered everything for the party. Well, he felt pretty sure.

"Panda, we forgot us!" Donkey shouted as the spaceship took off on its own, leaving Panda and her behind!

Panda used his remote control to bring the spaceship back to the ground. Then they climbed inside again, but Panda was starting to feel upset. "We're going to be late to the party, but I just don't know if I forgot anything else!" he wailed.

"**Think, Donkey Hodie, think,**" Donkey said to herself. How could she help her friend remember everything for the party?

Donkey looked around the inside of the spaceship for ideas. Then she saw the "Start the Spaceship and Blast Off" list.

"A-ha! I, Donkey Hodie, will help you make a list!" she said to Panda. A list helped Panda remember how to start the spaceship and blast off, so Donkey knew that making a list of things to bring to the party would help Panda remember everything he needed to bring!

Donkey pulled out some paper and a marker. "Okay, what do you need?" she asked.

Panda took a deep breath and started listing the items out loud. "Birthday card, birthday cake, party balloons, party horn—wow, it's a lot to remember," he said. "Making a list sure does help!"

They still had to pack many things, including the party ping-pong table, the birthday crown, and fuzzy birthday slippers. One by one, Panda gathered them all while Donkey checked them off the list.

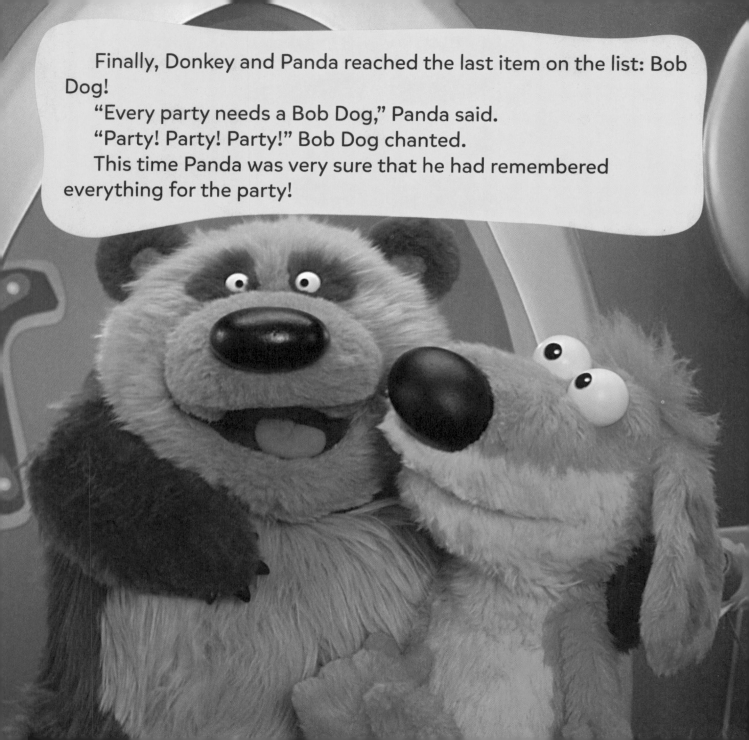

Finally, Donkey and Panda reached the last item on the list: Bob Dog!

"Every party needs a Bob Dog," Panda said.

"Party! Party! Party!" Bob Dog chanted.

This time Panda was very sure that he had remembered everything for the party!

Donkey, Panda, and Bob Dog buckled up, pressed the big purple button, and counted down:

3... 2... 1...

BLAST OFF!

"Planet Purple, here we come!" Panda shouted.
This time they made it all the way to Planet Purple without turning back! Donkey's list really helped Panda.

"Happy birthday, Mama Panda!" Panda shouted. He was so happy to see her!

Donkey, Panda, and Bob Dog cheered. Mama Panda was thrilled by her birthday card, birthday crown, fuzzy purple birthday slippers, and everything for her party. "How did you remember all these things?" she asked.

"We made a list!" Panda replied.

Then Panda, Donkey, and Bob Dog sang a special birthday song for Mama Panda that went along with the birthday card Panda drew for her.

Today is your birthday,
so we want to say
everything we love about you
on your very special day!

We love your warm bear hugs,
we love your purple hairdo,
we love your belly laugh,
we love dancing with you!

We love your purple smoothies,
we love your bedtime stories,
we love your smiley smile,
we love spending time with you!

Happy birthday, Mama Panda,
happy birthday to you!
Happy birthday, Mama Panda,
we're so glad you're you!

The birthday party was a big success, especially with all the things that Panda had prepared!

"Thank you for helping me remember everything for today's party," Panda said to Donkey.

"You got it, best pal!" Donkey replied, giving her best friend a big hug.